For Becca and all the staff and children at York Rise Nursery,

with love and thanks —R.H.

For Val —S.H.

Text copyright © 2007 by Richard Hamilton
Illustrations copyright © 2007 by Sue Heap

Typeset in Slappy Stevens
Art created with acrylic paints

First published in Great Britain in 2007 by Bloomsbury Publishing Plc
Published in the United States in 2007 by Bloomsbury U.S.A. Children's Books
175 Fifth Avenue, New York, NY 10010
Distributed to the trade by Holtzbrinck Publishers

Library of Congress Cataloging-in-Publication Data
Hamilton, Richard.
Let's take over the kindergarten / written by Richard Hamilton ; illustrated by Sue Heap.
p.   cm.
Summary: When their teacher gets stuck in the jungle gym, the kindergarten students
decide to take over the classroom and do exactly what they want—at least for a while.
ISBN-13: 978-1-58234-707-3 • ISBN-10: 1-58234-707-7
[1. Kindergarten—Fiction. 2. Behavior—Fiction. 3. Teachers—Fiction. 4. Schools—
Fiction. 5. Stories in rhyme.] I. Title: Let us take over the kindergarten. II. Heap, Sue, ill. III. Title.
PZ8.3.H1862Le 2007   [E]—dc22   2006040732

First U.S. Edition 2007
Printed in Singapore
1 3 5 7 9 10 8 6 4 2

All papers used by Bloomsbury U.S.A. are natural, recyclable products
made from wood grown in well-managed forests. The manufacturing processes
conform to the environmental regulations of the country of origin.

LET'S TAKE OVER THE KINDERGARTEN

Illustrated by
**Sue
Heap**

**Richard
Hamilton**

BLOOMSBURY
CHILDREN'S
BOOKS

Miss Tuck got stuck
in the jungle gym.
That was bad luck—
she won't do that again.

Because . . .

Oh, how we giggled
as poor Miss Tuck wriggled,
and little Louis cried,

Naughty Gemma locked the door.
"Grown-ups aren't allowed anymore!"

"Do what you like," cried silly Spike,
speeding around on a little blue trike.

"Children, children,"
said Miss Tuck.
"Stop this, please,
I'm really stuck."

Water, water, everywhere—
in our shoes and in our hair!

Sticky glue,

gloopy glue,

let us pour it

over you!

Paint the paper,
paint the floor,
paint the windows,
paint the door.

Paint your hands,
paint your face,
paint and paint
all over the place.

"Naughty children!" cried Miss Tuck.
(Then suddenly she had to duck.)

"Early lunch, I do declare!"
called Louis from the teacher's chair.

"Chocolate cake," giggled Fred,
standing nearby on his head.

"I know what," cried clever Clive. "Let's push the oven down the slide!"

"Time to learn,"  said Beverley. "A-B-C and 1-2-3.

Write your name,  sing a song,

do a dance,  bang a gong."

"Children, children, please be quiet.
This is a disgraceful riot!"

We were happy,
we were glad—
until things started turning bad.

Then Pip tripped Kip,
who hurt his lip.

And Milly and Tilly
got sat on by Lilly.

Molly and Polly
fought over a dolly.

And Tim pinched Kim
until he cried . . .

Miss Tuck was stuck,
but not for long,
because we kids
were mighty strong.

"Take my arm,
and 1-2-3,
pull **very** hard,
so I'll pop free!"

Hurray!

Up to Miss Tuck ran Tilly and Milly,

and Pip and Kip and Molly and Polly,

and Kim and Tim and tearful Rory.

She gave us a hug and read us a story,

and then everything was hunky-dory.